# Where's Eeyore's Tail?

Adapted from a story by Hallie Marshall

Illustrations by John Kurtz

You think you can depend on tails.
You don't expect tails to go wrong.
The last I looked, it was right there.
Now, when I look there . . . it's gone.

"Don't tell me," Christopher Robin said. "Just turn around."

Eeyore turned and Christopher Robin asked, "Where did you lose it this time?"

Eeyore shook his head sadly. "I have no idea."

Christopher Robin told Owl and
Rabbit about Eeyore's missing tail. While
Owl talked (and talked) about where a
tail might be (and where it might not),
Rabbit gathered his friends and organized
a search party.

Everyone joined in the search. From the tallest to the smallest, they combed the Hundred-Acre Wood.

The tail was not to be found.

And then Christopher Robin and Gopher accidentally fell into a deep pit.

Pooh and Piglet had dug that pit to try to catch a heffalump. It had been so long ago that everyone had forgotten about it. The trap was covered with broken branches and leaves.

As Christopher Robin and Gopher crashed through, Christopher Robin thought, I hope I don't fall on him.

The pals landed with a thump, but safely. Christopher Robin began calling, "Help! Help!"

Gopher stamped his foot a few times. "Ground's too hard for digging," he said. Soon Kanga and Roo and Tigger and Rabbit were there, then Piglet and Pooh and Eeyore and Owl. They gathered around the edge of the pit and looked down.

Christopher Robin looked up. "I think I could climb out of here," he explained. "But I don't believe Gopher can."

Roo had an idea. "I saw a piece of rope back there, all twisted in the thistles," he said. "We could use it to help rescue Gopher."

"Roo!" cried Christopher Robin, when Roo showed him the rope. "You've found Eeyore's tail!"

It *was* Eeyore's tail, and it ended up being very useful. They used it to pull Gopher out of the pit.

Christopher Robin got out of the pit by himself. Then he fastened Eeyore's tail back on.

Roo was a hero. They all yelled, "Hip, hip, *Roo*ray! Hip, hip, *Roo*ray!"

And Eeyore was especially happy as he wagged his very useful tail.